M000014312

What a Race!

by Amos Theodore
illustrated by Molly Windsor

Harcourt
SCHOOL PUBLISHERS

Printed in China

ISBN-13: 978-0-15-358470-1
ISBN-10: 0-15-358470-X

Ordering Options
ISBN 10: 0-15-358357-6 (Grade K Advanced-Level Collection)
ISBN 13: 978-0-15-358357-5 (Grade K Advanced-Level Collection)
ISBN 10: 0-15-360724-6 (package of 5)
ISBN 13: 978-0-15-360724-0 (package of 5)

5 6 7 8 9 10   985   15 14 13 12 11 10 09

Cat, Dog, Ox, and Bun will run.

They will have a race.

They get set to go.

There they go!

Look at Dog and Ox go!

Who do you think will win

the race?

3

Do you think Dog will win
the race?

Dog will not win.

Dog fell in a mud pit.

He has to get out.

Will Cat win the race?

She will run and run.

She can pass Dog.

She will come up to Ox.

Do you think Ox will win
the race?

Ox will huff and puff.

Cat can pass Ox.

Ox will not win.

Will Bun win the race?

A log is there.

That log is full of moss.

What do you think they

will do?

Bun will have to hop on top.

Cat will go on the moss.

Who do you think will win?

Who do you want to win?